Sex: A Bit Tricky
(and not always sexy)

Maggie Deveau

Copyright

DEDICATION

This book is dedicated to my family who love me unconditionally, to my partner who makes my toes curl every time we kiss, and to everyone who thinks about sex.

You are all amazing.

CONTENTS

ACKNOWLEDGEMENTS

I'd like to thank Chris for reading the roughest of rough drafts, Justin for pulling me through the scary no-man's-land draft in the middle, and Liz for doing the 'red pen' edits as we headed for the finish line.

xoxoxo

BS (BEFORE SEX)

I WANT YOU to think back. Way, way back in time. I want you to remember what it was to be on the cusp of womanhood. My, doesn't the term "cusp of womanhood" sound like a phrase that would come out of your mother's mouth? I'm thinking back to sixth grade when we were all 11 turning 12 years old. At this point in our pre-pubescent careers we had started wearing deodorant, whether we needed to or not, and we had all bullied our mothers into buying us training bras, whether we needed them or not.

Proudly we would thrust our chests out so that the triangles of our bras would press visibly against the cotton of our t-shirts, and we would cherish those days when our deodorant would "accidentally" fall out of our backpack in front of the whole class.

Oh my, how embarrassing, oh my, look at how grown up I am.

Have you made the mental leap back there yet? Can you feel the butterflies of anticipation playing in your stomach, as you wonder when, oh when, will I get my period? When, oh when, will I get to kiss a boy for real...with tongue? And how far should I stick my tongue into his mouth? What if he chokes? What if he gags and vomits? Oh gross!

But I digress. Let's jump into lunch hour and see what the girls are up to, shall we?

WE FIND FOUR best friends huddled around a notebook. This is a very important notebook. This is the book in which they have listed each boy from the class. The boys are weighed, measured and given a final score. We live in a democracy, and as such, each girl was allowed a vote, and the average scores of those votes were tallied on a scale of one to ten in "The Book".

Cutest. Nicest. Best Eyes. Best Lips. Funniest. Smartest.

One day, the book was discovered by the vice principal and disclosed to the entire class. The girls' parents were called. The young ladies were admonished and publicly humiliated. Apparently, having a secret was considered inappropriate. No amount of crying would sway the school from its decided course of action. The girls had to apologize in person to each boy whose name was listed in the book. In a class of thirty-six students there were about fifteen boys. Fifteen mortifying apologies that were followed up by the teasing and the torment that only young boys can dish out.

Our gang of dishonoured pre-teens learned a lesson. Not the intended lesson, but they did learn a lesson. Instead of instilling a respect for others, the adults had inadvertently stoked our ladies' imaginations. Why were the adults afraid of them having secrets? What was it the grown-ups were so afraid of them discovering? The lesson learned was both valuable and simple: if you have a secret, you lock that motherfucker up and hide the damn key.

And that is what they did.

A new book was born, and this one was far more interesting. They hid their new book in a security box under a bed. Once a week after school they would meet to fill its pages with the latest acquired knowledge. They were certain that there must be something really, really, dirty out in the universe that they weren't supposed to discover. Being unsure of what this terrible knowledge could possibly be, they decided to do some research. A library is a powerful oracle.

Judy Blume's book, *Are You There God? It's Me, Margaret,* was thrown to the wayside, and her much interesting book, *Wifey* was consumed in turn. They found a copy of *The Joy of Sex* in the non-fiction section, and hid it behind a collection of *Little House on the Prairie.*

When the first periods began to flow, these ladies were armed with knowledge. They no longer judged the boys on "cuteness" or "best laugh"; now their book was filled with hypothetical case studies.

"If Jason showed up at your door wearing nothing but a towel, would you let him do more than just kiss you?"

"How old should you be to lose your virginity and not be a slut? Fifteen, sixteen, or seventeen?"

Waiting for marriage wasn't even a consideration.

So many important questions came from these young women who had yet to suck on a boy's tongue.

Imagination is a potent tool. Every boy was pictured wearing nothing but a towel, or naked, or in ripped jean shorts, and it was assumed that all these boys would grow into men with bodies like Michelangelo's *David*.

I REMEMBER THIS time. I remember that in my own devious mind, I always pictured men dripping wet. They would be fresh out of a shower or standing bravely in the rain or better yet, riding a horse in the rain. I knew in my heart of hearts that wet men were sexier than the dry variety.

I never did get over that imagery as a sexy turn-on. As an adult, I still have to agree with my 12-year-old self that wet men really are sexier then dry men, and I applaud the wisdom of my virginal mind.

***

Oct. 31, xxxx:

We the undersigned, on this most powerful and magical night of Halloween hereby swear to guard the book of Soul Secrets with our lives. We promise never to tell lies in the book, and the book will keep our secrets. We promise to tell the truth and be the best of friends always. Anyone who breaks this oath will be cursed forever! We make this vow before God, Queen and our Country. We so solemnly swear.

Louise, Nancy, Maggie and Jenny

Amen.

FIRST KISS

EVERY GIRL'S FIRST kiss is a bit different. I invite you to remember the anticipation. Remember that moment when you didn't know if you should turn your head to the left or to the right. Should you link your hands behind their neck, or wrap your arms sinuously (a great phrase you read in your mom's Harlequin) around their waist? You have a split second to decide as destiny leans towards you with minty fresh breath and a new set of braces.

You close your eyes and damp, trembling, lips meet your own.

Objectively speaking, that first kiss most likely fails on the execution score. Enthusiasm, on the other hand, rates a perfect ten. Luckily, the memory doesn't care about objectivity. Emotions rule the memory of the first kiss.

After the kiss, you couldn't stop thinking about it. You relived every second of it on repeat in your imagination for days. That couldn't have been you out there, at a dance, kissing a boy in public! And so what if his braces cut your lip a bit? You were flying so high you were feeling no pain. You could handle the gossip. You were positive there was going to be gossip. Your first kiss was witnessed by hundreds of students on the dance floor. George wasn't even your date. He was supposed to be at the dance with Nancy, but she caught the flu, and George never asked her to the dance, but that didn't matter. Everyone knew George was supposed to go to the dance with Nancy. Instead, he danced with you. Okay, you asked him to dance with you…but you weren't expecting it to be a slow song! It's not like you had any evil intentions. He's a buddy of yours. You were being a friend. You were just being a good friend…right?

Instead of Nancy, he danced with you. He kissed you. And you noticed that after the kiss, you danced a lot closer to one another. You held each other just a little bit tighter than before.

The song ended. George looked at you; you looked at George. No words were spoken, and in that moment you felt totally grown up. Maybe you shouldn't have been the one getting the lip-lock, but you were in the right place at the right time. You, as a matter of fact, had a hand in your own destiny by being the one to ask George to dance. Good life lesson to hold on to: she, who asks for what she wants, gets it. Interesting!

Does the memory of your first kiss make you smile? Does your heart do a small flip for that one perfect moment in eternity when a boy or a girl really liked you, and you really liked them, and you kissed?

Admit it! You are smiling right now and a part of you wants to jump up and down and squeal just like you did when you told your best friend all about it over the phone that night. Did you write about it in your diary? How many pages did you fill? Three, Five, Ten pages of descriptive text and anxiety for the future?

Do you still have that diary?

I do.

***

How many boys have you kissed?

Louise:	Two! Paul in grade three and Mike from the public school last summer
Nancy:	Zero. And third grade doesn't count!
Louise:	Totally counts.
Nancy:	Totally doesn't! Maggie?
Maggie:	One, on the cheek, Sam, last year.
Louise:	Okay, cheeks definitely don't count!
Maggie:	Well, I kinda caught the corner of his mouth. Will that do?
Louise:	Fine! You get half a point, for half a kiss.
Jenny:	I'm going to kiss Tyler at the dance next week.
Maggie:	If a cheek doesn't count, then the future sure doesn't!
Jenny:	I kissed Nathan at the wedding last month.
Nancy:	Nathan, your cousin the usher? That Nathan?
Jenny:	Second cousin.
Louise:	EWWWWWWW!
Maggie:	Is that even legal?

VIRGINAL SEX

FAST FORWARD, IT'S time to lose our virginity. Some of us regret how it happened. Some of us don't. The first time you have sex is rarely an awe-inspiring experience, but it is often an educational one.

In 10th grade Kate met a boy in art class. He had blond hair, blue eyes and was just and inch taller than her at 5'7". In her world, he was perfect. He was also bit of a bad boy who'd recently started smoking pot. Kate didn't even smoke cigarettes, so weed seemed like a big bad wolf. Out of concern for him becoming an addict, she went so far as calling the Kids Help Phone line and couldn't figure out why the councilor on the other end kept laughing while she patiently explained that pot led to acid, which led to cocaine, which led to heroin, and a life of becoming a dealer and a pimp.

Oh Kate.

Anyway, her philosophy about virginity was that it was a nuisance that should removed efficiently with as little muss and fuss as possible. She figured that once she got the dreaded "first time" out of the way, she could go off to enjoy a life of fulfilling orgasms. Kate was certain there would be pain and no orgasm for her, so best to get it out of the way, mop up the blood (naturally she believed it would be of biblical proportion) and move forward as a woman.

Her one hard and fast rule was that she wanted to lose it to a man that she was "in love" with. Good thing Mr. Blond-hair-blue-eyes fit the bill. For simplicity's sake, let's call him "Bill", since he fit it and all. After dating Bill for about a month, Kate decided to pop the question and let him know that it was time to move forward with their relationship. They cut class and caught a bus to her house.

The two of them had been indoctrinated with safe sex lectures since the age of eleven, and as a result that poor bastard was informed that he would be wearing two condoms for this occasion. TWO Condoms, one over the other! No ifs, ands, or buts.

I wonder if he could feel anything.

Here's Kate's telling of the tale:

"SO THERE WE were in my bedroom, lying on my tiny twin-sized bed surrounded by pink wallpaper and stuffed animals. I was nervous as hell and couldn't stop giggling. We had come here for one purpose and one purpose only, and suddenly I didn't have a clue how to proceed. I'm honestly not sure how we managed to get to the naked stage of the program, but this part I will never forget: I was lying there under him and it was time to do the deed. I was so tight that we couldn't get it in, and I was so wired that I couldn't relax at all. He'd press against me and it would start to hurt and then we would stop.

"It was mortifying.

"After about three attempts I thought to myself, 'this is ridiculous.' I steeled myself against the pain, shut my eyes, bit down on my lower lip and gouged my nails into my palms. He managed to squeeze in there, and I'm not going to lie to you, it hurt like hell. There was absolutely no rhythm to the event. All that bullshit I'd read in books about "coming together as one" was obviously fabricated. If he moved up, I was down, if he moved left, I moved right.

"I tried to be sexy. He tried for longevity. We finished in less than three minutes.

"He went to the washroom to clean up and I sat on the bed, wondering how many times we would have to do this before I'd get an orgasm.

"Bill wasn't sure what to expect from me when he walked back into the bedroom. His friends had all warned him that he would have a crying, hysterical female on his hands. I must admit that a small part of me wanted to indulge in a bit of a cry, but the much larger part of me was quite smug. Bill wrapped his arms around me and told me that he loved me.

"I smiled at him and said, "Can we do that again?" and promptly fell into a fit of hysterical laughter as his jaw hit the floor. Hey, I just wanted a chance to cum.

"My virginity was gone and I was pleasantly surprised that it wasn't the traumatic experience I'd been indoctrinated to believe. I called my best friend and told her every gory detail. She was one of those adventurous types that always got to do everything first, and being as competitive as I am, I found that super annoying.

"Not this time. This time, I won. She was still a virgin and I was a woman! Nah na na nah na!"

***

January 15, xxxx:

We the undersigned hereby agree that none of us will lose our virginity until we are at least 17 years old, because then we will be in grade twelve and will know the difference between puppy love and real love. If anyone breaks this pact and has sex before they are 17, they owe everyone else $20.00 each! We make this declaration before God, Queen and our Country. We so solemnly swear.

Louise, Nancy, Maggie and Jenny

Amen.

COLLEGE

YOU HAVE SUCCESSFULLY navigated high school and are marching gaily into the world of post secondary education. These are going to be the most important years yet. You will get a degree/diploma/trade certificate. You will become a responsible member of society who makes shit pots of money. You will meet "the one" and you will live happily ever after. You will drink copious amounts of beer, be a liberated slut, and you will discover that every woman is but two martinis away from a girl-on-girl encounter.

WHAT? Oh yes my friends, we don't all admit to it, but the vast majority of us did a lot of exploratory surgery between the ages of 18 and 24. I understand you didn't do it on purpose, it's not like you were looking for it, it just kinda happened. Right? I mean there you were, all innocent-like: dressed up as a Girl Guide for Halloween while your friend Carrie was dressed up as a cop. She thought it would be fun to tackle you and handcuff you. As you lay there on the ground with your hands bound behind your back, you could feel Carrie's breath tickling the back of your neck and you got an irresistible urge to...

I want to do what, with whom?

You found yourself doing mental gymnastics for the rest of the day as images of her lips on yours, of your face buried in her breasts, continuously flashed through your mind.

Don't worry about it. You knew what to do. You called up your favourite boy toy, Sean, for a date, and informed him that you were going to give him the best sex of his life. You skipped your women's studies class that afternoon as you didn't think being encouraged to despise the male half of the species would be conducive to an evening of seduction. You ran home and prepared for battle.

You remember the mad dash of frenetic energy, don't you? Dropping your bags, shoes and clothes haphazardly in a path to the shower? Gathering your thoughts as you let the scalding water pour over your head as you washed, rinsed, and repeated as necessary?

You brandished your razor like it was a bayonet, as you dove into the trenches. Unfortunately for you, due to the never-to-be-spoken-of dancing-on-the-table incident last semester, you'd been on a sex moratorium, and thus your "garden of splendour" resembled a jungle in Vietnam.

Your plan was a simple one, and should have been easy to accomplish. Have sex with Sean. But when you showed up at the pub and your date was standing by the bar smiling at you, Carrie was there too. She was on the dance floor and you couldn't look away. You drank a pint or three of lager, ignored Sean completely, made a beeline for the dance floor, and started flirting outrageously.

When Carrie tilted her head to the right and ran one finger down your cheek to your collarbone it was game over. Without saying a word, you walked off the dance floor and left the pub together.

WOMEN ARE SOFT in all the right places, and there is something absolutely erotic about sharing a bed with someone who has the same physical make-up as yourself. In many ways this situation finally gives you the freedom to explore with uninhibited abandon, as you might not have done with a man in the room. This is body is like your body. This body is also insanely different from your body now that you are looking at it as an outside observer. You have played with yourself enough to know what feels good on you, but you are very aware of how difficult it is for someone who is not you to make you cum. What if she's the same? How in hell are you going to please her?

YOU WERE TERRIFIED when you first buried your face between her legs. She smelled amazing, and you couldn't lap up enough of that slightly salty, sexy, juice that was uniquely she. You prayed to God that you would get this "right". Growing up, you'd practiced kissing with your dolls, not spelling the alphabet with your tongue around an imaginary clitoris. You couldn't have practiced, even if you'd thought of it as an option. You weren't flexible enough for self-cunnilingus. None of your dolls were anatomically correct. You have had no training for this moment in your life. How are you not going to fuck this up?

Guess what? You didn't have to fly blindly in the abyss. She opened up her mouth and told you what felt good for her. Her voice gave you the permission to use your own. Up until that moment you hadn't realized how silent you were in the bedroom. How, because you were worried about hurting your man's ego, you stayed quiet instead of asking for what you wanted. Not this time. You found your voice and you used it. You spent a night flying between fucking and snuggling and making love and communicating and cumming...oh God the cumming and the touching and the tender and the hard. By morning you understood why the Goddess is worshipped.

I DON'T WISH to imply that you can't have great sex in a mature male/female relationship. I suspect most bad sex is just the natural outcome of ego, insecurity and a gross lack of communication. But we are talking about college here. Sex with most college boys is like fucking the Energizer Bunny on speed. You might remember the one guy, out of the many, that was surprisingly great in bed during the college years? You have fond memories of him. Remembering him tugs your lips into a small smile.

Your memories of Carrie, on the other hand?

They make you gasp, soak your panties, and touch yourself.

***

Would you ever kiss a girl?

Louise: No way! I like boys.

Nancy: Maybe?

Maggie: I don't know, wouldn't the breasts get in the way?

Jenny: My Mom would kill me. And how big do you think yours
            are going to grow anyways Maggie?

Would you ever kiss a girl and a boy at the same time?

Louise: I guess if the boy was into it.

Nancy: Maybe?

Maggie: I guess. But how? Are both their faces on one half of my
            lips at the same time?

Jenny: Maggie, don't be an asshole, you know we mean "make
            out".

Maggie: Fine, yeah I'd try it. Jenny?

Jenny: Nuh-uh, my Mom would kill me. She just knows things.
            She'd know and I'd be dead.

Louise: Chicken!

Nancy: Chill out Lou. So what if the boy wasn't into it?

Louise: And I made out with her? I guess he'd break up with me because he'd say I was cheating.

Maggie: Is it cheating if you're both girls?

Jenny: I have no idea.

FRIENDS WITH BENEFITS

THERE ARE GOOD days and there are bad days. This was a bad day. I hadn't had sex in a month. I know, I know, no sex for a month isn't that big a loss, but for Christ's sake, it sucks when the person that you are having sex with is in the same office with you, and is your friend, and you hang out all the time, and all you want to do is grab him by the lapels of his jacket and say "look ass wipe, if you don't fuck me right fucking now, I am going to kill you!" Well hell!

That's the problem when you start having sex with your friends. If the sex is even remotely good, you want to have more sex with them, but naturally they have "other shit" to deal with in their lives, so they don't necessarily want to have sex with you every day, or once a week, or once a month, or (help a sister out here) once every six weeks.

Please?

In an ideal fuck-buddy relationship you are both happy, mentally balanced, and can enjoy a flirtation without compromising the buddy-buddy aspect of the relationship. You should be able to grab a beer and shoot a game of pool together, or send out a quick text saying you need to rock out with your cock out, and all will be well-received and enjoyable.

You should not be possessive, or jealous, if the other person starts dating. You should be calm, cool, collected and hopefully, well-satiated. You should not be polishing your gun to kill the bitch that wants to get her claws into "your man". After all, he isn't really your man at all, is he?

Smooth sailing with your "Friend with Benefits" is rare. Inevitably one person begins to slide into a deeper emotional attachment then the other. I know this is sexist, but men seem to be a lot better at casual sex then women are. Ok, men seem better at casual sex than I am, and it seems to me it is most often the woman (me) who starts to get ideas about flowers, romance, candlelight dinners and "a future". Blame it on the chromosomal nesting instincts; blame it on Nora Roberts. I love your books, Nora, but seriously? Really?

Another pitfall of 'Friends with Benefits' is if both people begin having feelings for each other and they don't explore them. This hurdle occurs because the couple have set such firm ground rules on their fuck-buddy-ness that neither is brave enough to tell the other that their feelings have changed. They begin to bicker, cease communicating, and both suffer from eventual heartbreak. The relationship sours and they go their separate ways searching for new partners. If one of them had had the balls to speak up, they may have enriched both of their lives with a genuine relationship, and had some great sex too.

Relationships take courage, and so many of us approach our lives from a place of fear that we avoid risk at all costs.

You know you are truly friends if you can call each other on your shit, but still share a beer once the yelling has stopped. Some of these conversations are almost cinematic in their execution. I remember one such night that culminated on the streets of Toronto at top volume.

THIS DISCUSSION BEGAN, as many do, after a few too many drinks. It began quietly enough. We'd decided that it had been far too long since the last time we'd enjoyed a good fuck, and were making plans for the following Saturday night. I had company staying over the weekend, so it would be rude to do anything about our libido in the immediate future and I wasn't in the mood for a threesome with two guys.

The topic of COMMUNICATION reared its ugly head. I accused him of lying to me. He accused me of not being understanding.

"Why won't you talk to me?"

"Jesus Christ! It's not like you're my damn girlfriend!"

Tick, tick, boom! Months' worth of shit and repressed sexual frustration came pouring out of us in an incoherent argument that escalated to the point where we were yelling at each other, chain smoking and trying to force my houseguest to pick sides.

"Tom, do you hear this bullshit?"

"Um, I gotta pee. Excuse me."

Needing to cool off, but far from done with the venting, we stormed out of the apartment together to buy more cigarettes at the 24-hour convenience store down the street from where I lived.

"You done fighting yet?"

"No! You?"

"Not by a long shot."

"I've got a lot more to say and I'll be done when I'm damn good and ready."

"Me too!"

"Fine! Go!"

"Fine!"

He grabbed me, and proceeded to very angrily, kiss me senseless.

"I'm so fucking mad at you."

"I hate you right now."

"We're still fucking next Saturday, right?"

"Right"

"No matter what we say tonight?"

"Exactly."

"Good, 'cause I'm not done."

"Me neither."

"Fine!"

"Fine!"

Barking at each other like two angry pit bulls, we flagged a cab to take him home. We engaged in more kissing, groping and grappling then he jumped into the cab.

"See you Saturday?"

"Sounds good, looking forward to it."

"Fuck you!"

"And you!"

It was such a bizarre situation to find myself in that I kept wondering when I would hear the Director yell "cut" so we could set up for the next shot. It was so perfectly choreographed that I felt as if we were in the Mack-Daddy of romantic comedies.

FOR THE RECORD, we did get together the following Saturday and had a fabulous time. The screaming beast of my libido was fed, and our friendship was back on solid ground.

Just in time too, as shortly after that he re-entered the dating pool.

Even I fall prey to those "territorial" impulses. So much so, that the night he told me he was "dating" again, I took him back to his place and screwed him senseless. Talk about marking your territory. Sheesh!

MY EXPERIENCE BRINGS me to the conclusion that it is more mentally sound to keep your "Friend with Benefits" at a geographical distance. If you live far apart from each other, perhaps with a country or two between you, then it is a special treat when you do have a chance to get together. You fully expect the other person to have a separate and fulfilling life without you, on their own continent.

Then again, perhaps the term "Friends with Benefits" is the greatest misnomer of them all. If you've thrown in the benefits, shouldn't you just suck it up and call a spade a spade? Use the term lovers? You are already in a relationship: a friendship is a relationship. Hate to break it to you, but that's the truth. So either be lovers or don't. Being lovers doesn't require monogamy or orange blossoms, but at least you're not living a fabricated state of being every time you are together.

***

If you didn't love someone would you have sex with them?

Louise: No

Nancy: No

Maggie: Um, what if I really, really, liked them?

Jenny: No

Nancy: Seriously, why would you have sex with someone you didn't love?

Would you ever have sex with a friend?

Louise: Maybe. I love my friends so it would still be sex with someone I love.

Nancy: No, once you have sex you're no longer friends, right? You're like boyfriend/girlfriend and that would ruin everything.

Maggie: Yes. If he's my friend then he won't hurt me.

Jenny: No. I don't want sex with my friends. I want to save it for the really special guy. Like the one I might marry.

Louise: But you will have sex before you get married, right?

Maggie: How else will you not totally suck on the wedding night?

Jenny: No. If I fall in love, it will be real. And even if we have sex first, that's still the one I'm marrying.

Maggie: Well if I don't fall in love, then I'm going to lose my big V with a friend.

Jenny: You wouldn't!

Maggie: I would! I totally would, but not until I'm like 17. I don't have $60 just lying around to pay you guys!

Jenny: I don't think money should be part of your decision, Maggie.

LOVE

S ITTING DOWN TO write this chapter, I wasn't sure if I should be listening to endless Top 40 Ballads or Heavy Metal for inspiration. I kept gravitating towards Metallica, and that was perhaps a bad sign. Do I, of all people, attempt a diatribe about the ins and outs of love?

Sure, why the hell not?

We all have our opinions, so I might as well explore mine.

I am one of those people who believe in Love with a capital "L", True Love. And as such an individual, I have been questing for it most of my life. I am also hardwired to nurture, so I constantly run into the danger of setting my own needs and desires aside to prioritize the needs and desires of the one I am with.

I was a disaster in my twenties. Glad that phase of my life is over.

When I was a child, I knew exactly what I wanted in a man. He had to have blue eyes, had to like animals, make me laugh, and love playing and running around in a park. If he enjoyed the swing set and the monkey bars it was the ultimate bonus. I'd worship at his feet if he could play baseball and let me play First Base or Shortstop. He couldn't be more than two inches taller than me as I hated having to crane my neck up to look at people. He needed to hold my hand and would want to kiss me all the time. He had to have a wild grin that made me wonder what mischief he might be up to. When I was in elementary school, this was my ultimate mate. I wasn't worried about his financial status or his career goals. If he happened to grow up to be Han Solo or Indiana Jones, then all the better.

23

I had my first kiss in first grade. That blond-haired, blue-eyed boy kissing me on the cheek is one of my sweetest and most treasured memories. Naturally we were mortal enemies for the rest of elementary school. Our classmates never let either of us forget that one moment in time. But my untried heart would swell each time he would forget himself and speak to me. I knew that someday, we would be running from enemies in the jungles of the Amazon, we would be successful archaeologists / dinosaur hunters / rock stars / movie stars / racehorse breeders and we would have two beautiful children.

When I was in Jr. High, I just wanted a boy to like me. To really, really, like me. If he was cute, so much the better, but I just wanted someone to walk to the store with me at lunch for Slurpees and chocolate bars like all the cool, popular girls. I wanted someone to ask me to the dances. I wanted a guy who didn't mind that I had short curly hair and pink glasses. I wanted a boyfriend who thought it was cool that I read books and used big words. I wanted a guy that was so cool his coolness would rub off on me, and then everyone would like me. Maybe I would become wild and dangerous and tantalizing. Just maybe I would surprise them all.

I had my shortest relationship in Jr. High. He asked me out in the first class of the morning. I began weaving fantasies about first kisses, marriage and children through the next class, and then he dumped me right before lunch. What heartbreak! What a crushing blow to my hormonally fragile ego. I was later informed that anyone dating me would be committing social suicide. Social suicide! What a confidence builder!

High School was where I discovered my first true love. I'd undergone a serious makeover involving contact lenses, growing my hair long, a new wardrobe that no longer sported mint green pants, and joining a new crowd. I cultivated my image the way a spy cultivates a cover identity.

I practiced my new "seductive" voice. What a disaster! I thought I sounded like whisky and cigarettes, a 1920's speakeasy sexy. When I gasped out, "hey hon, how was your day?" to the cute boy at the mall, I just knew he'd melt into a puddle at my feet. I stared deeply into his eyes with mine half-closed in a sexy, slumberous manner.

"Are you feeling ok?" he replied, "Your voice sounds like you have a cold and your eyes are all fucked up."

The path to sexiness isn't without pitfalls and embarrassment.

That first slide into love, on the other hand, was glorious. Queasiness in the stomach, difficulty catching your breath, loss of appetite, these are the symptoms of first love...or disease. Talk about "knock you on your ass" conditions. The world sang with you. Nothing could defeat you as long as the two of you were together. You could overcome anything. You could kiss for hours. You were seriously considering losing your virginity. Then you stopped considering it and did the deed. Why not? After all, you were going to be together FOREVER!

Or not.

The hard fall out of love also has symptoms. Every time you saw him you would feel queasiness in the stomach, have difficulty catching your breath, and suffer a loss of appetite. These decidedly similar symptoms had a completely different effect on your heart. Instead of joyous anticipation, now everything hurt. Brushing your teeth in the morning felt like you were getting ready for the gallows. How were you going to face him at the smoking doors? Thank God you only had one class together! He probably wouldn't be there anyway as he would be too busy skipping class with his (gulp) new girlfriend. Ouch!

Thank goodness you had your best girlfriends around you to keep you drunk, high, laid and distracted while your heart slowly mended itself in time for the next climb up the ladder and slide into love.

ADULT LOVE. What is adult love? This is a challenging question. Truthfully, I have no idea how to define it without minimizing it or sounding trite. By the time we are emotionally mature enough to have a "real" relationship, we've already accumulated baggage. Some of us have started to feel a bit jaded and bitter. Once you've hit your thirties, you and many of your friends will have been in some serious long-term relationships, perhaps married, perhaps divorced, and perhaps still not having found true love. If you had found what you were looking for, you wouldn't be single, now would you?

Have you been picking bad partners, or is there something undeveloped within you that you haven't addressed yet? Now that's a question that can keep you awake at night. 4:00 a.m. is the worst. Why does introspective insomnia have to happen at 4:00 a.m.? Doesn't your stupid brain realize that you have to get up and ready for work at 6:00?

I sometimes wonder if we, as adults, try to layer too many demands on a relationship. Now the partner has to be financially solvent, well-balanced, well groomed, understanding of your needs, understanding the dynamics both as a couple and as single individuals, be perfect and not make any big mistakes. Add to this our dreadfully short attention spans and need for immediate gratification, and we have no patience for developing a relationship, or a mutual understanding, or working through issues and remembering that we are all flawed. We want the whole fucking trip right fucking now, and we have absolutely no tolerance for the speed bump called "life" that comes along with the ride.

I believe that this may be another example of six-year-old me being smarter than the current me. Maybe I should go back to my first ideal mate who had to like animals, make me laugh, and love playing and running around in a park. He'd hold my hand and kiss me all the time. We'd play on the monkey bars and his wild grin would keep me wondering what mischief was coming my way.

Only now I will adjust my expectations a little and say that eye colour doesn't matter and if he has any hair left on his head at all, it's icing on the cake.

***

Our top 10 most romantic movies of all time!

Grease

Splash

The Pirate Movie

Casablanca

Gone With the Wind

Pretty Woman

The Bodyguard

Beauty and the Beast

West Side Story

Gigi

ADULT SEX

THE BAND THE Pursuit of Happiness once wrote, "Adult sex is either boring or dirty".

...Yup.

THE WORKPLACE

I F YOU ARE lucky, 37.5 hours per week are dedicated to work, but for many it is 45 or 50 hours. I was once an Executive Assistant with most of my day spent on a computer. We EAs are creating spreadsheets, drafting documents, reviewing PDFs, sending emails, booking flights, and supporting our CEOs. At lunch and by the water cooler we complain that there just aren't enough hours in the day, the week, or the year. How does that bastard expect us to handle the insane workload that he dumps on us? How much more efficient can we possibly be?

I beg to pose the question...

What are we really doing with our day?

We are on the Internet.

We are shopping for exotic cheeses, snooping on social networks, laughing at YouTube and insta-chatting. You can lose a lot of day in an online chat. The topics are not how you are going to improve yourself or the world. They are often bitch sessions about a spouse/lover/ex/friend/potential, and they occasionally devolve into the racy, the fantastic, the sexual, and the dream life we don't get to lead when surrounded by beige and green cubicle walls lit by the fluorescents glaring down at us.

I wonder if all of our complaints about work are just an elaborate cover-up for the exciting fantasy life we lead while we are there. I mean, who really wants to go home to a pack of squalling brats and a lazy son of a bitch of a husband, when you could spend your day here, in the internet?

11:14 AM

Jane: *Hello there.*

Jon: *Hi.*

Jane: *You cozy in your bed?*

Jon: *Just getting in.*

11:15 AM

Jane: *Ok, I'll grab a coffee and be right back...I need to be prepared :)*

Jon: *Ok.*

11:17 AM

Jane: *I'm back. Get comfortable.*

Jon: *Yay. I am.*

11:19 AM

Jane: *Good, because today they came to him. Pandered to him, begged his favour, but today was not a day he wished to be disturbed. He lay back in his ornate bed, glass walls surrounding him on all four sides and waited for the show to begin. His handmaiden sat demurely beside the bed in a red and black satin robe waiting for instructions. "Keep your robe on...I don't want to look at you yet," he said.*

As the first screen opened on the glass wall to Jon's right, the handmaiden slipped her hand under the sheets. Framed in that first window was a woman bound and gagged over a desk, ass thrust into the air.

The screen over the second glass wall opened. Here was a woman blindfolded with her arms tied above her head, her feet barely touching the ground.

Jon, let me know when you've caught up on the reading.

Jon: *Are you alone there?*

Jane: *Not exactly alone - my boss is in the boardroom.*

11:26 AM

Jon: *Caught up. I like this one...*

Jane: *The third screen stayed closed, the second room dimmed and the lights came up brighter in the first.*

A woman entered wearing a loose-fitting shirt and a pair of black dress pants. Her hair was pulled back from her face, and she strode confidently towards the bound woman.

She placed one perfectly manicured hand on the base of the woman's neck and seemed to be murmuring lovingly into her ear.

11:31 AM

She then dug in and raked her nails from the base of the skull down to the woman's ass...

Jon: *Oh...*

Jane: *Four perfect rows, welling up gently with blood.*

Jon groaned at the sight of the red running into rivulets down the woman's ribs and his handmaiden began to gently fondle his balls.

The bound woman moaned.

11:35 AM

The dominant then reached into the cupboard nearby and withdrew a set of three balls strung together.

They glistened silver in the light.

She stepped behind the woman, and starting at her tailbone, slowly licked up the base of her spine...blood staining her lips, as her left hand spread the Sub's cheeks wide.

Stepping back she popped the balls in. One. The girl whimpered...no lube you see...

Two. Bigger now, wider...

Jon: *Mmmm.*

11:38 AM

Jane: *Three. The largest. As a courtesy, the Dom spat on this one before rolling it in.*

Tears leaked from the Sub's eyes but her hips began to pump against the desk's top.

"Would you like me to let you cum?" asked the Dom.

Nodding frantically the Sub ground into the desk.

"Well I won't." and with that she untied the Sub from the desk and made her stand on her own two feet, legs spread wide.

Her quim dripping, she stood shaking as one by one the Dom slowly removed the balls from her ass.

Meanwhile, in Jon's bed the handmaiden wrapped her hand around his cock and began to stroke it slowly. Up, down, squeeze, release.

The Dom turned from her subject, looked at Jon through the glass, directly in the eyes, and smiled knowingly as the lights dimmed.

"You can show me your tits now," he said to his handmaiden, "but only your tits."

She squirmed out of her robe so that it fell to her waist keeping her most intimate areas covered.

11:50 AM

The lights came up on the second room.

11:51 AM

"Keep stroking. Add some spit would you?"

She obeyed.

The blindfolded woman in the second room was cold.

11:52 AM

Her nipples were taut and hard as glass.

11:53 AM

Jon: *???*

Ooohhhhh.

11:54 AM

Jon: *Sending you a pic...careful...*

Jane: *K.*

OMFG!

Nice rod!

Jon: *Thanks...finish me off...*

11:56 AM

Jane: *She dangled in the second window, her arms already turning a slight bluish tinge from being so long suspended.*

The waiting, the not knowing, had her overheated and terrified.

Two men entered.

One dropped to his knees in front of her and lifted her legs over his shoulders as he engaged her clit with his mouth.

The second man stood behind her and reached around to fondle her breasts.

Pluck, twist on a nipple.

11:58 AM

Lick, bite on the clit.

She got wetter and wetter and Jon couldn't take his eyes away.

Even the glistening tips of the men's dicks fascinated him.

11:59 AM

"Mouth on me now," he commanded as he wrapped his hands around the maiden's head and locked them into her hair.

He pulled her down between his thighs and held her there as she gagged and gasped between strokes.

12:00 PM

Jon: *Ohhhhh.*

Yes.

Jane: *In the room the suspended woman started to keen...a high-pitched wail as her body bucked and shivered under the ministrations of the two men.*

12:01 PM

She drew closer and closer to the edge...her wrists raw from tearing against the restraints.

The man in front pulled himself to his feet.

12:02 PM

Locking eyes with the man behind her, he gripped her waist, lifted her hips and they plunged together inside of her.

She screamed from pain and pleasure as she came.

Jon:　*Yum.*

12:03 PM

Jane:　*She sprayed and dripped and sobbed and moaned as both men took their pleasure from front and back.*

At the last moment they both pulled out and shot their cum onto the glass wall...splattering it and defiling it as they had the suspended girl...the lights dimmed on the second room.

The third window remained closed.

Jon thrust hard into her mouth...but it wasn't enough.

Young, nubile...virginal...he wanted inside her.

Jon:　*I want to cum.*

Jane:　*He wanted to fuck her.*

Jon:　*Yes!*

Jane:　*He pulled her down and flipped her to her back, spreading her open.*

12:06 PM

She was soaked, her eyes glazed over in confusion and longing.

He placed himself at her center and thrust with no regard to her

35

sensitivities.

He felt the barrier of her innocence press against him and tore through it.

Locking her legs back over her shoulders he took her with no heed to anything but his own pleasure.

12:08 PM

She was tight, almost painfully so. Her eyes rolled back into her head as he thrust and plunged and played his own tip on her clit and then thrust again.

Jon: *Ohhhhhhhhhh.*

12:09 PM

Jane: *And again, so close, God he was so hard he thought he'd die before cumming and then…*

…He ripped out of her, drenched her face and hair with his seed, and collapsed.

12:10 PM

Jon: *I'm cumming. Yeah....mmmmm.*

Wow.

Thank you.

Jane: *You're very welcome.*

I'm jealous...at least you get to cum, I have to sit here at my desk all afternoon.

Hey give me 5 minutes...sorry work thing.

Jon: *No worries. I'll be around.*

1:11 PM

Jane: *Sorry, got held up. You still around?*

Jon: *I'm here.*

Jane: *Did it make you really hot or only lukewarm...and what was your favourite part – parts?*

1:13 PM

Jon: *It made me really hot.*

The only thing was that the chat kept on getting interrupted, that sucked a bit. The only one I didn't like as much was the woman tied up so her hands turned blue.

I loooovvvved the handmaiden.

1:15 PM

Jane: *Because her hands were numb or because she was being pleasured by two men?*

Jon: *Her hands were numb.*

Jane: *You're such a softie ;)*

1:16 PM

Jon: *Tee hee.*

Jane: *It makes me laugh that you have no problem essentially taking out a virgin, but you feel bad because a girl's hands were numb.*

Jon: *But the nails digging in and blood was real nice!*

HA!

That's me.... a bastard.

But a gentle one.

1:17 PM

Jane: *Aren't you glad you stayed home from work today?*

1:18 PM

Jon: *I am glad I stayed home.*

 Very glad.

1:27 PM

Jane: *I wonder what's behind window #3?*

Jon: *Tee hee.... tease... are you going to tell me later?*

1:29 PM

Jane: *You know, I'm not quite sure that I know what's behind window 3.*

 A paramedic maybe for your poor handmaiden? Ha ha!

1:31 PM

Jon: *HAHA!*

 I wouldn't be that rough on her.... although she might be gasping for air.

1:34 PM

Jane: *I figure she was passed out cold by the time you gave her the cream soda.*

Jon: *Cream soda. Nice.*

 I kinda like the thought of her being passed out...hmmm...what does that say about me?

1:35 PM

Jane: *It says that we are both sick puppies who need to get laid more often!*

Jon: *AGREED!!!!!*

HOW MUCH WORK do we do at work? I leave that decision to your conscience...and your libido.

***

Would you ever talk dirty to a boy to make him cum?

Louise: So he's jacking off? Yuck. No thanks!

Nancy: Do I have to see him doing it? Or is it like, over the phone?

Maggie: I don't know. What I would say? I'd feel stupid.

Jenny: I would. It's better than getting pregnant.

Maggie: Do you think there might be a book we could read?

PROSTITUTION

PROSTITUTION, STRIPPING, AND PORN are "hot button" issues no matter which way you undress them. One side of the issue paints the working girls as used, abused entities with all of their choices ripped away from them. The other side says that the sex industry can be quite liberating if working in it is a choice. I know women from both sides of the spectrum. I've seen the ones who are "pimped" and lose the majority of their income to their "managers" and to drug abuse. Yes this is horrific, and it is a tragedy, and a solution needs to be found, and no, I don't know what the solution is.

I've also seen women who treat the industry as a business, don't do drugs, and successfully manage their money, their real estate and their love lives. These women, in my opinion, appear no more mentally fucked up than anyone else I've met. They have more social obstacles to overcome as they are immediately judged for their profession, but the basic human needs, wants and desires are the same.

There is a third side to the sex industry that appears to be completely legal and socially acceptable, and is, in fact, encouraged by many responsible members of society.

What is it, you may ask?

The answer should be obvious. Marrying for money. Marrying for status. Marrying for security. Men and women have been doing it since the conception of marriage. Dowries, titles, land transfer, and political power have all had a hand in marriage.

If you are married and are becoming angry with me right now, perhaps you fall into this category? Are you married to a man with money? Does he grant you a place to live, a car, a nice credit card, and in return you warm his bed and appear on his arm at social events? Hate to break it to you sister, but you are now a whore. Ok, not a whore. Whores have lots of sex but make no money. You are a prostitute. You are getting paid. Hopefully you are being paid well.

The only difference is you are stuck with one man and a really messy divorce if things don't work out. Pimps take everything away when they drop one of their girls. You, fortunately, can hire a lawyer to try to keep some of your…earnings – depending on your pre-nup.

I hope that you are a high-class escort and are not just hanging out at "Hooker Harvey's" with the rest of the rabble. If you are high-class, then you probably live in a LARGE home and have multiple vehicles. If you are a streetwalker, you've probably settled on a man with a job and are still struggling to make ends meet. You have as many problems as you did when you were single, but now you have to deal with his shit as well. He pays the rent…Whoopee doo dah! Time to move up, woman!

I know I sound angry, but it just frustrates the shit out of me to hear these "liberated" women speak from their lofty place on high at the country club. They claim to be independent feminists but they are being taken care of by a man. These housewives of "what-ever freaking county" accuse girls with less money of being repressed by the patriarchy because they choose to wax; yet their own husbands are paying the plastic surgery bills. They hypocritically speak of the sanctity of marriage while having affairs with the pool boy. They look down their noses at strippers while taking pole-dancing classes every Wednesday night. They think prostitution should be illegal, when in fact they are Calvin Klein, Manolo Blahnik-wearing…ahem.

I don't care what you choose to do with your life. Just please, don't be a hypocrite about it. Throwing granite in Swarovski residences just isn't cool.

If there is consent between adults and it harms none, I say go forth, and do as you will.

Just please don't judge anyone else for their choices. And yes, I recognize that a big chunk of this diatribe was me appearing a wee bit judgmental about the judging. I am human; I am flawed.

***

Would you ever marry a man for money instead of love?

Louise: No!

Nancy: Maybe, how much money?

Maggie: Why can't you have money **and** love?

Jenny: No I wouldn't. You can't have money and love Maggie, because you have to be super mean to be rich.

Louise: That's stupid! Where did you get that idea?

Jenny: My Dad explained it to me when we saw the movie, *Wall Street.*

Maggie: That makes no sense, I'm sure there are rich people out there who are nice. There's got to be, or why would anyone hang out with them?

Louise: Because they are rich, duh! That's the whole point! You don't have to be nice or handsome or anything if you are rich.

Nancy: Hold on now, I have to not have love and he's ugly? Forget it! I'm changing my answer to a hard no!

Jenny: I'm telling you, love conquers all; marry for love and it will all work out. It's sorta like magic how it all works.

Maggie: What if I'm the rich one? Then it doesn't matter. I can marry a poor guy because I love him.

Louise: You can't do that. You can't make more money than him.

Maggie: Why not?

Louise: He'll hate you.

VACATION SEX

VACATION TIME IS precious time. You may have two weeks a year or you could be a lucky bastard and have three or more weeks per year. Many people don't take vacations at all. If they aren't working, they aren't paying the bills. I reiterate, "Vacation time is precious time."

Many of us try to cram absolutely as much fun as humanly possible into this minimal amount of time. We want to party, we want to relax, we want to sightsee, we want to meet new people, we want to be left completely alone, we want to drink, we want to eat, we want to be social, we want to be solitary, we want to play with our kids, we want to have time away from our kids, we want to do all this and more in x-number of days! We're going to make enough memories to last a lifetime, even if it kills us. The potential in our vacation rolls us out of bed in the morning. The fantasy of "what could be" keeps that smile plastered on our faces as our boss tears us a new one for something that is someone else's fault entirely. The chance to get away from "real life" is the drug that entices even the worst handler of money to save some of it. You can't buy a car, but by God, you will save for that all-inclusive to a tropical paradise in the middle of winter!

Can't save a dime?

That's why God invented Visa.

And God bless those hotel vacation reps that are there to serve your every need. Are you feeling ugly? They will tell you you're beautiful. Want a sexual adventure? How big of an adventure can you handle? Never done cocaine? That can be arranged. Don't believe me? Go to

Mexico.

I want you to close your eyes.

Visualize your vacation.

PICTURE HIM LYING in a large Jacuzzi tub, head resting back, eyes closed. The bubbles are frothing around you; a breeze is coming in from the open window, cooling your face, keeping you from feeling too warm. You've both had a couple of beers and are enjoying that slightly disjointed buzz that comes with the beginning of full body relaxation. He feels the water shift and froth as your legs slide up the outside of his and your breasts brush up against his chest.

You kiss him. Your tongue is pulled slowly and insistently from your mouth and suckled. A low throaty laugh, more of a memory of sound then sound itself, skips across your senses.

That is your laugh.

You didn't know you could sound like that. You didn't know a laugh could hold such intent. He goes instantly hard and the need for release begins to thrum in your blood. He reaches up to pull your wanton body to his, but you resist.

"Just stay still," you whisper, "just feel."

Reluctantly he allows his arms to drop back into the water and he takes a deep and stabilizing breath.

You arch back and tilt your hips. The folds of your center are just kissing his tip. He can feel you clenching and releasing around his head but not sliding down. He tries to rise up to meet you and to penetrate, but you rise up higher on your knees and deny him access. On a giggle, you shake your head, reach down, and cup his balls. Your hands are slick from the soapy water and you massage him, rubbing, tickling, and then withdrawing your hand. You place your left hand against the side of the tub for balance and your right between your thighs. Spreading the folds of your sopping wet pussy you find your clit, engorged, pulsing, wanting, and so sensitive you can barely put pressure on it.

He is holding himself absolutely still. You look him dead in the eye and begin the long slow descent onto his shaft. You take him inside you inch by inch, allowing your body to stretch and welcome him in. You smile and begin to move.

You are wild.

You are free.

IMAGINE THE CONVERSATIONS you could have with your best friend when you get back!

"The lasagna was amazing and then he fingered me in the cab! The cabbie was not impressed!"

"Then he said to me, 'if we're going to do this, we're doing it right, and I will be the best lover you ever had.' I called him a cocky bastard!"

"It was some of the most fabulous sex of my life."

"I've coined a new word, Cockcaine. Yeah, I snorted it right off his dick!"

"Damned for a penny, damned for a pound."

"And then he said, 'look at me, stay here; you are with me, just look at me.' Couldn't you just die from the romance?"

"I came 17 times!"

"He'd hold me as if I was the most precious thing in the world to him, and then bring me to peak with animal intensity."

"He massaged me head to toe with oil. With the sex and the heat and the oil and the sweat we slid and slipped and were a gooey slimy mess. We just kept rubbing and grinding into each other. We'd slide right off of each other only to climb back on to ride some more."

"You know what takes coordination? Sex in a hammock."

Those sure sound like fun conversation starters, don't they? They could be yours. You just have to go for it. Give yourself a chance to live a fantasy.

Pack a box of condoms and go exploring.

***

What are the coolest places to have sex?

Louise: How about a jungle? It's exotic and you don't get cold because you're near the equator.

Nancy: Too dangerous. You'd get eaten, or stung, or poisoned, or roll into quicksand and die. How about a beach?

Maggie: Sand gets everywhere. I swear there's still sand in my bathing suit drawer from last summer. It never goes away. Also don't you think it'd hurt? What if he gets sand on his, you know, and then scrapes you all up inside?

Jenny: Jesus Maggie, you're so graphic. Yuck. What's wrong with using a bed?

Nancy: Anyone can use a bed! Think special occasion sex.

Jenny: Fine! Um, a hot tub? Then when you're done, you're still clean because of the chlorine. Then you don't have to take a shower after.

Maggie: Yes you would. You don't want to go to bed with chlorine all over you. Your skin would drive you crazy, it would be so itchy.

Louise: And your hair, Jenny! Without conditioner, you'd wake up in the morning looking electrocuted. That's not sexy!

Jenny: But he loves me. So he shouldn't care what I look like, right?

Nancy: Um…

Maggie: Well…

Louise: Maybe just have sex in the shower instead of the hot tub?

Maggie: Jenny, that's perfect! Then you can have great sex **and** great hair!

Jenny: Ok…I guess.

WOMAN'S BEST FRIEND

FTER A YEAR of long-distance emails, text messages and sporadic visits, Ben and I were finally living in the same city. This deep attraction and insane sexual appetite for one another would be given life. My dripping wet panties would finally highlight anticipation instead of disappointment that fulfillment was out of my reach.

The week I arrived was filled with dinners and movies and Shakespeare and lovemaking and sex. Soft sex, hard sex, the type of sex that makes you melt, and the type that makes you scream. A body so well-used gets exhausted, so this day was going to be mellow. We decided to eat in at his place and spend the following day letting our dogs, Sandy and Max, romp around in off-leash parks. The scene was cozy, homey. I'd made homemade raspberry pie, which we polished off while drinking wine around the backyard fire pit. Our dogs lazed about without a care in the world.

I went inside to brush my teeth, slither into a slinky black negligee, and await his arrival in the bedroom so that I could love him thoroughly from the top of his head to the tips of his toes. He entered the room. My lover. The man I had been sliding into love with for a year.

"Come here baby," I purred, "let me take care of you."

"I adore you. You're perfect. I don't want a relationship with you."

I stood up and found myself in front of him, my only armour a black negligee, my dignity in tatters at my feet.

"I…what…I don't understand," I choked out.

Ben proceeded to tell me that he thought he was dead inside, and didn't have the ability to love. He told me that "on paper" I am the perfect woman for him. That if I was to hand in a resume about myself, he would have no logical reason to not love me.

"On paper? A resume? Are you insane?"

"Look," he said in the type of tone you use to quiet the mentally ill, "you've been drinking, it's not safe for you to drive home. You can stay here tonight, I'll make love to you one last time, and then you can leave in the morning."

Tears were pouring down my face. My breath caught in my throat, I was gasping for air like an asthmatic. My heart was pounding, slamming against my rib cage. My thoughts were scattered across the universe and I couldn't pull them back together. I was somehow separated from my body and couldn't make it obey my mind. It was then I felt the warm furry presence of my dog Max pressed up against my leg. His low continuous growl cut through the chaos and I felt myself slam back into my body. The tears still fell, but there are many types of tears. Max's growl became my growl.

"You ate my pie."

"What?" he asked.

"You ate my raspberry pie."

"It was delicious?" he took a step backwards to place some distance between us.

I stepped forward. I was angry. I think I might have gone a little mad.

"You ate my God-damned raspberry pie. You do not eat a woman's pie and then break up with her. You DO NOT let an evening get to the point of lingerie and then break up with her. You fucking coward! A real man would have at least had the balls to face me when I was fully dressed. Not wait, until I am here, like this, mostly naked, half drunk and in bare feet."

I wasn't shouting. I was too angry. I was too sad. I was righteously indignant. I was the low growl that had grown louder from the throat of my Max. I had my wolf pack with me, and this mongrel dared to stand alone in front of us? His dog, his overbred dog, his dog that did not know how to be a pack, was nowhere to be seen.

I calmed myself, schooled my features into a mask of gentle entreaty. I reached one trembling hand up to caress his cheek.

"I'm sorry. You're right; I've been drinking. I'm not thinking straight. I can stay? You'll make love to me one last time?"

"Yes, baby. Yes. Let's just settle down and go to bed."

I looked down at Max, he looked at me, and I looked dead into Ben's eyes. A sharp smile cut across my face and I lashed him with my voice.

"I guess you've never heard of a taxi either, you fuck."

Max calmly walked over to him, lifted a leg and pissed all over Ben's feet.

"What the hell?"

"You ate my raspberry pie, asshole. Good dog, Max," I patted his furry little head, "good dog."

I grabbed my jeans, my shirt, my purse, my good dog, and we walked out the front door and caught a cab.

***

April 22, xxxx:

We the undersigned *hereby agree to the following:*

We will not be the ones who get dumped. We will dump him first.

We will break up with him face-to-face.

He will never see us cry.

He will never hear us beg.

We will throw a sleepover party for the recently single girl and eat lots of ice cream.

If we are older than sixteen, we will drink champagne with our ice cream.

We make this declaration before God, Queen and our Country. We so solemnly swear.

Louise, Nancy, Maggie and Jenny

Amen.

CUMMING TO AN END

I HAVE THIS recurring dream. I'm laid out on a large bed. It is an extremely large bed, bigger than a king. It's also extremely high profile. I'm stretched out on this bed and I'm cold. All that is covering me is a thin draping of gauzy white material. My nipples are so tight from the cold and irritated by the feel of the cloth, they hurt. My legs are spread and bound to the posts at the foot of the bed. I can feel the breeze from the overhead fan tickling my labia. I'd love to scratch, but my arms are also spread and my hands are bound to the posts at the head of the bed. I squirm about in an attempt to avoid the breeze.

Right about now is when He enters. Sometimes He looks like someone I used to know. Sometimes He looks like the Tenth Doctor. Mostly He doesn't have a clear face. I have the impression of dark hair, dark eyes, lips that look like they are frequently tense and rarely allowed to smile. I get the impression of a man whose control is like a tightly coiled spring. I'm scared of what would happen if the grip on that control ever slipped. He is fully dressed. He looks ready to dine at a five-star restaurant. As He approaches the bed and I see his height in relationship to it, I understand.

"Hello. Let's get you ready for dinner."

At this point I realize that I can't speak. Not because I'm gagged, I'm not; I am truly mute. My eyes widen in panic as his hand comes towards me. I try to squirm away into the mattress.

"You chose to be here, now let's begin."

I chose to be here? I chose to be bound on a bed at the whim of a stranger? Why can I not remember why I would choose to be here?

Now would be the time to panic. I'm not panicking. Okay, I'm panicking a little, but certainly not enough for the situation at hand. Why?

He starts by hooking a finger in the material that covers me and slowly drags it down my body. This further irritates my nipples and they grow even more erect. The cloth tickles my arms and I feel goose bumps dance across my skin. The cloth slithers across my belly; a gentle weight on my mound. It blocks some of the wind from the fan, so my clit gets a chance to relax. It is a relief to not have the air blowing against me. I am almost calm.

His head lowers and I feel his tongue flick across one nipple and then the next. He then opens his mouth and takes in my left breast. Bathing it with his tongue. Sucking it, teasing it, massaging it with his lips. I can't take my eyes off the top of his head. He has so much hair. His hair is thick and black, wavy and unkempt. It's quite at odds with the severity of his face. I close my eyes. I start to drift on the sensations. Each time He pulls at me with his teeth; I feel it echoed in my core. Dampness is pooling between my legs. I'm climbing; I'm yearning. My hips begin to rock of their own accord. What little weight there is on me from the pooled cloth across my hips, I'm trying to use to seek release.

He pulls himself away from me.

"I think not."

There's an acute and painful pinching.

I'm pulled right out of the river of pleasure I'd been drifting on. My mouth opens to yelp, but no sound comes out. I stare down at my left nipple and there's a bright silver clamp attached to it. I look up at him. A quick blade of a smile cuts across his face and the second clip being clamped to my right nipple zaps a shock through me that sears all the way down to my toes.

QUITE OFTEN, THIS is where I bolt awake in bed. Covered in sweat and feeling phantom pains across my skin and shadows of the orgasm that never happened throbbing between my legs.

IF I DON'T wake up, the dream jumps ahead and I am at the dinner party with him. I'm wearing a sheer evening gown of black chiffon. I know that He has dressed me himself, but I can't seem to remember any part of him doing so. All in attendance can see the clamps on my chest, the chain that connects them, and the chains that dangle to my clitoris, where one more delicate silver clip is nestled between my folds. It's difficult to walk without sending shocks of pain across my nerves. Every motion pulls or twists. The fabric of the gown catches on the delicate links of the chain, causing me even more trauma. I am taking the tiniest steps I possibly can.

He stops at the head of the table and all of his guests sit. All of his male guests sit. Where are the women? Why is there no chair for me? I feel the pressure of his hand on my right shoulder as He pushes me, not unkindly, but very firmly, to a kneeling position. There is a crystal bowl on the floor filled with champagne.

"Drink."

As carefully as I can, I bring my face down and begin to lick and suck the champagne. I've begun to acclimatize to the pressure on my nipples, but the agony on my clit just cannot be blocked out. The wine goes straight to my head and I feel giddy. This isn't so bad, really. There's a cushion under my knees, so at least there is some small comfort afforded to me. As dinner progresses, He feeds me bits of everything that He is eating, so I am not hungry. Every now and then He strokes my hair. I am a beloved, cherished pet. I can make it through dinner.

He bends down and whispers in my ear, "I owe Number Four a favour. Suck his cock. Now."

I find myself under the table, between Number Four's legs. Number Four is unpleasant. He's loud and obnoxious. Four is currently devouring his dessert of crème brûlée and bragging about his prowess in business. His member is already out of his pants. Just waiting for little old, unlucky me. As I wrap my lips around him, he places one hand on the back of my head and guides me down. Number Four is so deep into my throat that I'm gagging and fearful that I might vomit across his lap. In and out faster, and faster he rams my head over and over into his lap. I can hear the conversation continuing above me. His dialogue hasn't broken stride. There is no indication that he is fucking some woman's face under the table. He asks his neighbour to pass him the coffee as his cum splashes into the back of my throat.

I lay there on the floor under the table, in pain, shaking, and still dry heaving, as I taste the residual bitterness in the back of my throat. I'm too weak to crawl back to my place. I just want to lie down and sleep.

The dream skips again. He's brought me back to the bed where everything began. He's so pleased with me. He says I was a very good girl and that I can have my reward. He pulls me to the edge of the bed where He is standing, and enters me slowly. As He begins to move inside me, He removes the clamps one at a time. The relief is a new type of pain; it is so intense. As the last clip, that most painful clip, is removed, a wave of unadulterated bliss washes over me. My libido screams, I wrap my legs around his waist and drag him towards me. I rock hard into him. I hear myself scream as my voice comes back to me. I've got control of the rhythm. I'm cumming. I am cumming so hard. I rip myself off his cock and arch back as He comes across my stomach and tits. I splay my hands across my body and massage all that has spilled onto me, into my skin. A sticky soothing balm. I grab my mound, rub hard, and cum again.

I wake up.

I wake up and if we're being completely honest, I wake up, fuck the hell out of myself and cum at least three times.

THE IMAGINATION IS such a fabulous and potent tool. When you are in your imagination things hurt only as much as necessary to turn you on. Things that you don't necessarily like in "real life" are just good fun in your fantasy. Dreams are so utterly delicious and fucked up.

I read somewhere that sex dreams aren't really about sex at all, unless of course they really are about sex. Alrighty then. So sometimes they have nothing to do with sex and other times they have everything to do with sex. Honestly, as long as they lead me to an orgasm, who cares?

You know what is fun though? Reaching into those dreams and trying bits and pieces of them in real life to see how they fit. That's how I found out that I really hate the taste of pee, regardless of how well chilled the glass. It's also how I found out that I really love…well…that's for me to know.

***

Dear Diary,   *May 22, xxxx*

I've never written a diary before. I love my friends, but I don't think they always understand me. Today, in the book, we were voting on what kinds of sex we wanted to have once we were married. Our choices were Penthouse sex, snuggly sex, being the boss sex, or being the office girl sex. I said that I want to have all the different sex with my husband and Louise said I'd never get that with only one person. Each man likes one type of sex, she said, so I had to pick just one type of grown-up sex. She said if I wanted more than one type, I'd have to have sex with lots of men and that that would make me a cheater. My other choice was to never get married, and die a lonely, childless, slut, but at least then I wouldn't be a cheater. Then she kept calling me "Maggie the cheater" all day.

She even turned it into a stupid song.

> *Little slut thinks she's so neat*
> *But all she does is cheat cheat cheat*
> *Her husband's not the only one*
> *She's sucked and played on just for fun*

I hate today. I hate all of them today. No one was on my side. They made me feel like a monster. Louise is supposed to be my best friend. She was just kidding around, right?

When I got home, Mom asked why I had a bug up my bum. So I asked her if being with Dad forever was boring and if she ever thought about other men. Mom freaked out! Like she really freaked out. She said that "alley catting" around makes you an unfaithful wretch and a bad person. She said, "It doesn't matter if you get bored. Marriage isn't about excitement."

I've never heard Mom so hard and mad. Not even when I broke her favourite pair of heels when I was trying them out last summer.

Then she demanded to know why I was asking. I couldn't tell her what really happened, or I'd be betraying my friends, our pact, and our book. So I lied and told her I overheard older boys talking on the bus.

"Words are important, Maggie," she said. "You have to be very careful of the words people associate with you. They will define you, and how people see you. You never want anyone to associate bad words with you. Ever! You're a nice girl. Just be nice."

I don't want to grow up and have people think I'm a bad person. I don't want to be a cheater or a lonely slut. There's got to be other options? Right? If it's impossible to do all the sexing with only one person, what's going to happen to me if I pick the wrong person and he likes one type of sex and I like another kind? Divorce?

Mom would kill me if I got divorced.

How much sex am I going to have to have before I get married, to make sure I'm not going to be a cheater? And if it's more than two or three guys, won't that mean I'm a slut anyway?

Thank God I lied to the girls when we were talking about our dreams! We were supposed to write down our dirtiest dream in the book. I wrote that Jason came to my house and I answered the door wet from a shower, wearing only a towel. I wrote that I let the towel fall to the floor and that I let him grab my breasts and kiss them. Jenny thought I was soooo badass. I can't imagine, after today, what they would have said if I'd shared a **real** dream with them.

See Diary, I keep having these dreams, and I'm a different person in each dream. I do different things depending on which person I am. Sometimes I'm helpless and I've lost my voice. Sometimes, I'm like Wonder Woman and I have the guy tied down with my magic lasso. Sometimes, I even dream that I'm a man and I'm the one with a penis. Maybe I need to see a psychiatrist? I wake up feeling really weird. Like I've almost found something, but I can't quite grab onto whatever that thing is. I'm a bit scared of the dreams, but also excited. I can't wait to close my eyes at night and watch the movie in my mind even if it hurts my chest and I feel like I can't breathe and my tummy is all fluttery. If any part of these dreams is true, I don't know if I can get married, not if I can only do one type of sex, one way, forever! I don't think I'm strong enough. I'm scared that I am a cheater and a slut.

Those are such ugly words.

Cheater. Slut.

Mom's right. Words are important and they do define you and I'm not a cheater yet. I'm not a slut yet. I have time to find a better words and to become better words. You'd think it would be easy. Mom said to be nice. But I'm not so sure I want to be nice either. That word feels wrong and makes me sad.

People say I'm smart. That's their word for me. Smart. And because of that, teachers don't pick on me much, even when I don't know what I'm doing. They just think I already know the solution and I'm giving some other kid a chance to answer. So maybe that could be the word.

Smart.

But that word sounds like a brat or a know-it-all, and smart people get picked on. I need to be clever enough to avoid that.

Clever.

Peter Pan was clever. "Oh, the cleverness of me!" That's what he said. I got an 'A' on that book report.

I'll grow up to be clever. I'll grow up to be smart enough that I can figure out how to try all the sexing and clever enough to not let anybody know that I get to have all the sexing. No one will ever know and then they won't call me the bad words.

They'll just call me Maggie because they'll have no idea how clever I really am.

And I will have all the sex.

CLEVER

AND I WILL have all the sex. Thank God for that. Imagine the relief that young girl felt when she discovered that humans weren't one-dimensional. The relief she felt, once she discovered people could enjoy more than one type of "sexing", was a tidal wave of joy. There was hope, that if she did ever get married, she would not be bored to tears!

Oh the cleverness of me that I chose not to be 'nice'. I invite all of you to avoid being nice. Did you know that in Middle English, nice meant stupid? Did you know that the word derives from the Latin *nescius,* which means 'ignorant'? Don't believe me? Google it or go to a library and look it up the old fashioned way. Seriously, who wants to grow up labeled stupid or ignorant? I certainly don't, do you?

Sex is tricky isn't it? There are so many voices that surround us. There's so much noise! Noise from your parents, your friends, your faith, your work, and your own mind, all contribute to lost opportunities and lost orgasms. We're programed from a very young age to behave, to be nice, to follow the herd. You know what happens when you follow the herd? You flail off a cliff like a buffalo or a lemming. Do not despair. Unlike the buffalo or the lemming, you have a great big frontal lobe in your head and are capable of thought beyond prey or migratory-based behaviours. Our beautiful brains create fiction. We have imaginations. We are capable of complex thoughts and ideas. I feel that our brains are sorely abused. We take all this noise into our skulls, and instead of creating something distinctly, uniquely us, and distinctly beautiful to us, we transform information into hideous monsters. We give those monsters a life of their own, and the strength to block us from achieving our dreams and our desires.

Look back at those young girls. Wouldn't it be easy to diminish their experiences as naïve, or stupid, or foolish, or ignorant, while looking back at them from the high horse of adulthood? Those young ladies were fearless in their exploration. Truly they were quite brave. They were exploring their world to the best of their abilities with the tools they had at hand. When was the last time you took a good hard look around you, and explored your world, your thoughts, and your dreams without censure? You have so many more tools than they did! Why do we settle for status quo when we could be exploring and experimenting and growing? Our biggest crime as adults is to confuse the youths' lack of experience with a lack of insight. There is much wisdom to be gained, if we can cut through the noise of however many decades it's been, and see ourselves for a moment as we once were.

Touch a finger to your lips. Trace your lips. Inhale and close your eyes and remember when you would imagine what a kiss would feel like before you had ever had the chance to kiss. Bake the sensation into your brain. Go home and kiss your lover with the same gentle exploration you just gave your lips. Inhale, close your eyes, breathe your lover in and let it be the essence of the first time you ever kissed. I use the word essence, because you are using your imagination to create this moment, this new moment that is the child of innocence mixed with experience.

Ask yourself some questions. Which of your views have changed, which have not, and why? I let my view on what I wanted in a life partner be affected for years because of the noise around me. I let outside opinions on what was "right" or "grown-up" govern who I was looking for in a mate. I let myself grow so far away from child-me that I almost ended up in an abusive, sexless marriage. I was getting older, and I was told that I should be grateful that anyone would want me. I believed them when they said I should be grateful anyone would tolerate my "quirkiness".

I had locked up that clever little girl who was once me. I had abandoned her and her diaries and her questions. I ignored her scratching and her imploring at the door of my psyche for years, until one day, when I was broken, she broke through. She was confused and dismayed by the state of affairs in my relationship, and she certainly didn't recognize me as coming from her.

"Does he make you laugh?"

"Go away."

"Does he love playing and running around in a park?"

"Stop."

"Does he hold your hand and kiss you all the time?"

"Stop."

"I wanted all the sex! Where is the sex?"

Where indeed was all the sex? Why weren't we running around a playground having a blast? Why weren't we having sex in the playground for Christ's sake? That would be the best of both worlds wouldn't it?

"You are not clever. You are just nice!"

Ouch!

I never locked her up again.

Now comes the tricky part of not getting stuck back there. After all, you certainly wouldn't be engaging in the full spectrum of adult pleasures you have available to you, if you are only guided by child-you. Child-you, after all, is the same person who couldn't wrap their head around the concept of "dirty talk". Child-you believed that Olivia Newton John and John Travolta were the ultimate in romantic love. Child-you was also a bit of a dumbass about money and traditional gender roles. Also, you didn't clue in to the fact that Gigi was being groomed by her grandmother to become a courtesan until you were twenty. So what does that say?

Now is the time to engage those enlarged brains and explore the imagination. Grow. Change. This isn't a permanent contract. You don't have to like the same things for the rest of your life. You might adore anal sex in your twenties, and hate it in your forties. That doesn't make it right or wrong. It was what felt great, for you, at the time.

There are enough people out there who wish to control your behaviours, without you adding more censure onto the pile.

Be cool about who you are.

Be cool with what makes you hot.

Be cool with your comfort and your danger zones.

How you feel about a thing may very well change as time goes by. Friends become lovers, lovers become friends, things heat up and they cool down. Moods can shift daily. Some days, I feel I am the sexual Goddess of the universe. Then there are days where I am wearing sweat pants, and the only thing I'm eating out is a bag of chocolate chip cookies. Believe it or not, there are even times I can't stand the thought of sex and that's ok too. Some days I'm too stressed out to cum, and on others, all I need is a good stiff breeze to tip me over the edge into happiness.

What turns you on today is hilarious tomorrow. Having a sense of humour is the key. Every time your imagination slams into reality, the comedy is exponential. Embrace it!

The first boy who kissed you? Twenty years later you find yourself having brunch with him and his husband.

The first woman you ever made love to? Married a man.

Is your best friend from the academic challenge program a university professor? Nope. She's the lead guitarist in a Goth band in Germany.

Remember your religious studies teacher, Mrs. Cardinal? Well she is the proud owner of your favourite sex store, and gave you a 25% discount on the We-Vibe you bought yourself for your birthday last year.

Embrace the absurdity and enjoy the laugh. Life is too short not to laugh.

I want you to have fun. I want you to explore your sexual world. I want you to believe that there is nothing wrong with your imagination. I want you to know that you are amazing! My final words to you are to just get out there and enjoy a fabulous, consensual world of sex, without judgment, and without causing harm.

Sex. It's a bit tricky. It's not always sexy. But it's the best bang for your sweat equity buck in the amusement park we call life.

The End

ABOUT THE AUTHOR

Maggie Deveau is a lover of humans and believes that they have the utmost, untapped potential to be amazing. Her parents forbade her from watching violence and horror on television when she was growing up, which is why she had nightmares for weeks after seeing "Halloween" for the first time in her twenties. Side note, "Tucker and Dave vs. Evil" just might be the most brilliant film ever made.

The bright side of living through the trauma of television censorship, is that young Maggie was allowed to watch as much sex and love content as she desired. This exposure has led her to be ridiculously optimistic, curious as a cat, and delightfully adventurous in her real life.

A BIG THANK YOU TO ALL YOU AMAZING READERS OUT THERE!

www.ingramcontent.com/pod-product-compliance
Lightning Source LLC
Chambersburg PA
CBHW020918180626
46816CB00007BA/2465